Snow Ghost

For Doris, Bob & Rowan – T.M.

For H and M – always my inspiration – D.M.

BLOOMSBURY CHILDREN'S BOOKS
Bloomsbury Publishing Plc
50 Bedford Square, London, WC1B 3DP, UK
29 Earlsfort Terrace, Dublin 2, Ireland

BLOOMSBURY, BLOOMSBURY CHILDREN'S BOOKS and the Diana logo are trademarks of Bloomsbury Publishing Plc

First published in Great Britain in 2020 by Bloomsbury Publishing Plc
This edition published 2021

A catalogue record for this book is available from the British Library

ISBN 978 1 4088 7662 6 (PB)
ISBN 978 1 5266 0537 5 (eBook)

1 3 5 7 9 10 8 6 4 2

Printed and bound in China by C&C Offset Printing Co., Ltd.

FSC
www.fsc.org

MIX
Paper from
responsible sources
FSC® C008047

To find out more about our authors and books visit www.bloomsbury.com and sign up for our newsletters

Snow Ghost

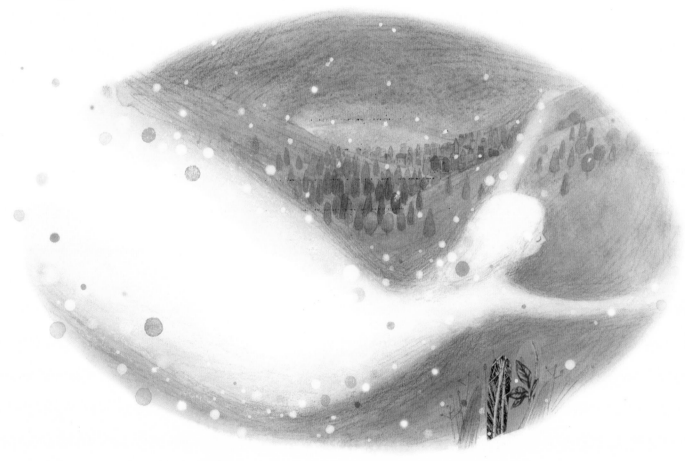

Tony Mitton

With illustrations by Diana Mayo

BLOOMSBURY
CHILDREN'S BOOKS
LONDON OXFORD NEW YORK NEW DELHI SYDNEY

Snow Ghost came shimmering out of the air,

searching for somewhere to settle –

but where?

She needed to find the place that was best,
a home to be happy, a shelter to rest.

When she caught sight of the lights of the town,
their glittery twinkling soon drew her down.

But as she grew closer,

what she felt most . . .

was, nobody there would welcome a ghost.

Snow Ghost went searching across the dark sky,

but its cold, empty loneliness

caused her to sigh.

She made her way into

a dense, tangled wood . . .

she'd find a home there if only she could.

But the darkness and shadows were gloomy and eerie,
so Snow Ghost flew on, feeling tired and weary.

A breeze blew her up to the top of a hill,
where the ease of the air filled her up with its thrill.

But how to find rest, where the chilly winds blow
and endlessly murmur,

Be off with you – GO!

Then . . .

high on the moors – a small country farm!

Could this be the place to find safety and calm?

Outside, in the field, were a girl and a boy,
catching the snowflakes
and laughing with joy.

They were playing at snowballs and running about,
and the winter air rang with each
whoop and each shout.

So Snow Ghost swooped down

with a swish and a swirl . . .

to join in the games
with the boy and the girl.

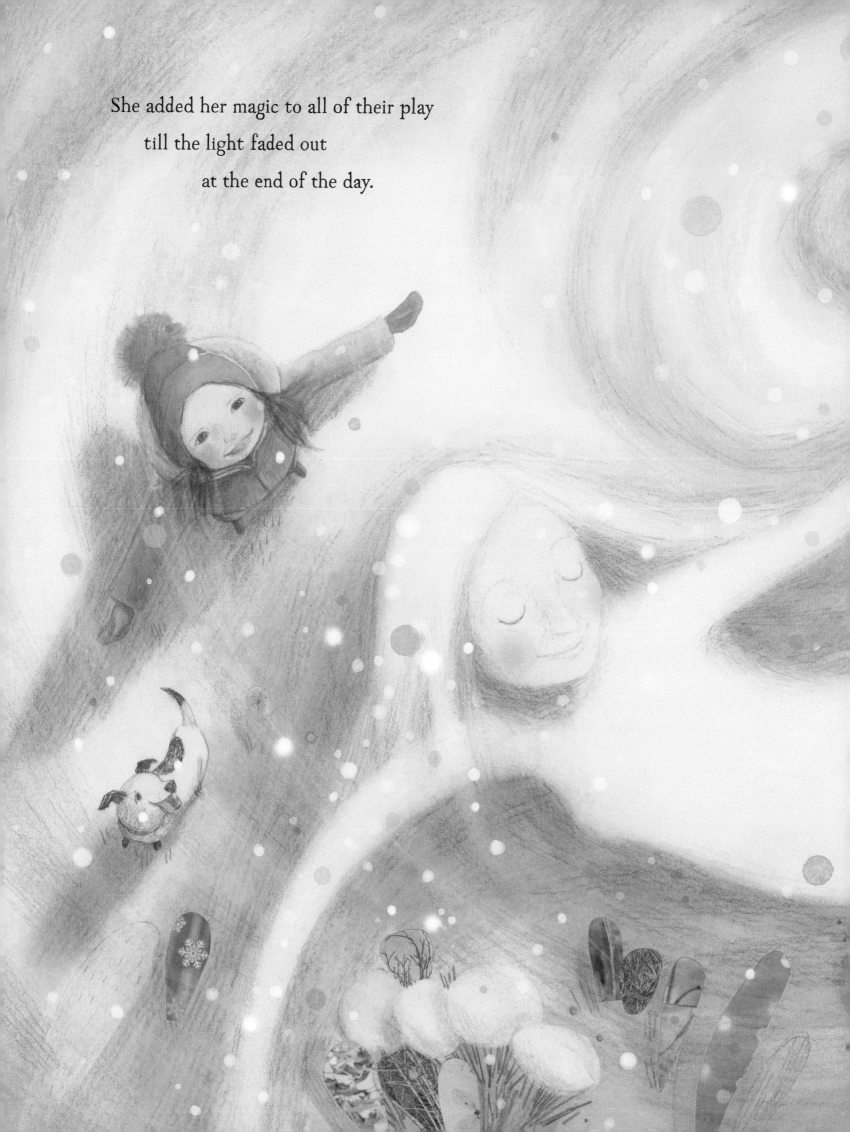

She added her magic to all of their play
till the light faded out
at the end of the day.

And she knew that she no longer
needed to roam,
for here was a place
she at last could call home.

A voice called the children, "It's time, now, for bed!"
and they both stumbled in with a tired, weary tread.

It was time for *Goodnight* to their magical friend –
time for the whooping and snow-fun to end.

The boy and the girl, through the cold evening air,
looked back at Snow Ghost and waved to her there.

And they knew in their hearts, as she settled to rest,

that Snow Ghost was home,

in the place that was best.

So while the soft moon shone its silvery light,
for Snow Ghost the world
was now steady and right.